Welcome to ALADDIN

If you are looking for fast,
with colorful characters, lots of kid-friendly
humor, easy-to-follow action, entertaining
story lines, and lively illustrations, then
ALADDIN QUIX is for you!

But wait, there's more!

If you're also looking for stories with
tables of contents; word lists; about-the-
book questions; 64, 80, or 96 pages; short
chapters; short paragraphs; and large fonts,
then **ALADDIN QUIX** is *definitely* for you!

ALADDIN QUIX: The next step between ready
to reads and longer, more challenging chapter
books, for readers five to eight years old.

Read more ALADDIN QUIX books!

A Miss Mallard Mystery
By Robert Quackenbush

A Miss Mallard Mystery

CABLE CAR TO CATASTROPHE

ROBERT QUACKENBUSH

ALADDIN QUIX

New York London Toronto Sydney New Delhi

ALADDIN QUIX
Simon & Schuster Children's Publishing Division
1230 Avenue of the Americas, New York, New York 10020
This Aladdin QUIX paperback edition September 2019
Copyright © 1987 by Robert Quackenbush
Also available in an Aladdin QUIX hardcover edition.
All rights reserved, including the right of reproduction in whole or in part in any form.
ALADDIN and related marks and colophon are registered
trademarks of Simon & Schuster, Inc.
For information about special discounts for bulk purchases, please contact
Simon & Schuster Special Sales at 1-866-506-1949 or business@simonandschuster.com.
The Simon & Schuster Speakers Bureau can bring authors to your live event. For
more information or to book an event contact the Simon & Schuster Speakers Bureau
at 1-866-248-3049 or visit our website at www.simonspeakers.com.
Designed by Tiara Iandiorio
The illustrations for this book were rendered in pen and ink and wash.
The text of this book was set in Archer Medium.
Manufactured in the United States of America 0819 OFF
2 4 6 8 10 9 7 5 3 1
Library of Congress Cataloging-in-Publication Data 2019931556
ISBN 978-1-5344-1415-0 (hc)
ISBN 978-1-5344-1414-3 (pbk)
ISBN 978-1-5344-1416-7 (eBook)

First for Piet and Margie,

and now for Emma and Aidan

Cast of Characters

Miss Mallard: World-famous ducktective

Inspector Willard Widgeon: Miss Mallard's nephew and inspector for the Swiss police

Madam Merganser: A famous opera star

Tilly Pintail: Madam Merganser's wardrobe mistress

Chester Gadwall: Madam Merganser's secretary

Philip Merganser: Madam Merganser's husband

What's in Miss Mallard's Bag?

Miss Mallard has many detective tools she brings with her on her adventures around the world.

In her knitting bag she usually has:

- Newspaper clippings
- Knitting needles and yarn
- A magnifying glass
- A flashlight
- A mirror
- A travel guide
- Chocolates for her nephew

Contents

1

Stolen Jewels

On a ski holiday in the Swiss Alps, **Miss Mallard**, the world-famous ducktective, went to visit her nephew, **Inspector Willard Widgeon** of the Swiss police.

The two detectives went skiing

together on Mount **Catastrophe**. But Miss Mallard did most of the skiing because her nephew hated the cold. He liked staying close to the fire in the lodge on the mountaintop.

"Sure you won't join me?" asked Miss Mallard every time she started out to the slopes.

Willard just shook his head no.

"Very well," Miss Mallard always replied. **"QUACK-A-LAY-EEE-HOO!"**

And off she would go again.

One afternoon there was a sudden snowstorm. It snowed so hard that the Mount Catastrophe **cable car** service was halted.

Inspector Widgeon had to spend the night in the mountaintop lodge. Miss Mallard had reached the foot of the mountain when the storm came. She stayed at her nephew's house in the village during the storm.

When morning came, the storm had ended. The cable car was running again, and Miss Mallard

set out to join her nephew.

Miss Mallard got on the empty cable car with her skis and knitting bag, where she kept her detective tools and news clippings. Slowly, the car started up the mountain. Miss Mallard held on to a strap and looked down at the wintry scene.

Soon the cable car was passing the winter **retreat** of the famous opera star **Madam Merganser**. Through the large picture window Miss Mallard could see inside.

"Good heavens!" cried Miss Mallard. "What's going on in there?"

Miss Mallard peered through the glass. She saw Madam Merganser tied up and **gagged** on the floor.

A robber wearing a ski mask was taking jewels from the wall safe. Then the cable car moved on, and the window was out of sight.

"Oh dear!" Miss Mallard cried.

Miss Mallard waited **anxiously** for the cable car to reach the mountaintop. She wanted to tell her nephew about the crime she had just seen.

2

Robber on Skis

"Now I see why they call this place Mount Catastrophe," Miss Mallard said to herself.

At last the cable car reached the top of the mountain. Miss Mallard ran to the lodge.

She found Willard where she had left him—warming his tail feathers in front of the fireplace. She told Willard about the robbery.

"We must go there!" she cried. Inspector Widgeon looked at the roaring fire and then back at his aunt.

"All right, Aunty." He sighed. "First let me see if I can find an extra sweater."

Miss Mallard helped her nephew put on as many coats and

sweaters as they could find. Then they went out and raced down the mountain—the first skiers in the fresh snow.

When they got to Madam Merganser's, Inspector Widgeon said, **"Look!** The robber has escaped! The front door is open, and there are fresh ski tracks leaving the house. They are heading toward the village."

Miss Mallard and her nephew peered along the single line of ski tracks. The robber was nowhere in sight. So they took off their skis and ran inside.

They found Madam Merganser where the thief had left her.

Quickly they untied her and removed the gag from her beak.

As soon as she was set free, Madam Merganser let out an ear-piercing scream:

AYE-EEEEEEEEEEEE!

It was the highest quack she had ever sung in her singing career. It shook the house and sent a huge pile of snow sliding off the roof.

"Feeling better?" asked Inspector Widgeon when she stopped screaming. "Now tell us everything you know about the robbery. Mind if I add another log to your fire?"

"Please do," answered the opera star as she started to tell her story.

3

A Missing Ace!

Madam Merganser said she had been alone in her house since yesterday afternoon. Just before the storm, her wardrobe mistress, **Tilly Pintail**, and her secretary, **Chester Gadwall,** went to the village to stay overnight with friends.

At the same time, her husband, **Philip Merganser,** went skiing. He got caught in the storm and fell, breaking his leg. He had to have his leg put in a cast. Then he took a room at the Hotel Edelweiss to wait for the storm to end.

"So I was a sitting duck for a robbery this morning," said the singer. "I had just opened my safe to put away some papers when in burst the robber."

"I saw the crime from the cable car," said Miss Mallard. "We got here as fast as we could."

"Was the robber a male or a female?" asked Inspector Widgeon.

"I don't know," replied Madam Merganser. "No words were spoken, and the robber was well disguised by a ski mask."

Just then the telephone rang.

RING!

RING!

Everyone jumped at the sound! Madam Merganser answered the phone. It was her husband, Philip. She told him about the robbery.

"Don't worry, Philip," she said. "Detectives are here making a report. But do hurry home."

Madam Merganser hung up the phone and turned back to Inspector Widgeon and his report.

"I really have no other information to share with you," the

opera singer told the inspector. "Perhaps you should leave now."

Meanwhile, Miss Mallard had found some playing cards on the table. She flicked through them.

"Why is one of the **aces** missing from this deck of cards?" she asked.

"I don't know," answered the singer.

"Hmmm," said Miss Mallard.

When Inspector Widgeon finished filling out his report, Miss Mallard asked, "Shall we follow

the robber's tracks to the village, Willard?"

Inspector Widgeon moved closer to the fireplace. "But, Aunty, who will stay with Madam Merganser?" he asked.

"You will, of course," said Miss Mallard, smiling at her nephew.

Then she turned to Madam Merganser. "Where are Tilly Pintail and Chester Gadwall staying? I would like to ask them a few questions while I'm in the village."

"Here," said the singer as she wrote down the addresses. "When you see them, tell Tilly and Chester to come back here at once."

4

A Snowy Clue

Miss Mallard took the addresses, went outside, and walked over to her skis.

It was so cold, she couldn't blame her nephew for staying inside next to the warm fire.

With skis on, Miss Mallard began following the robber's ski tracks. She had gone only a little way when she saw something!

She bent down and picked up two pieces of paper. One was a dated **receipt** from a drugstore. The other was a dated receipt from a hardware store. Both papers showed that items had been bought the day before.

A little farther on, she found one more clue. It was the ace from Madam Merganser's deck of cards!

As Miss Mallard followed the robber's tracks, they began to **merge** with other ski tracks—for skiers were now out on the slopes.

She looked around to see if one of the skiers might be the robber. But they were all wearing ski masks, so it was impossible to know.

As the skiers whizzed past her, Miss Mallard looked at the tracks they made in the snow. The tracks reminded her of something. Then she remembered what it was.

"Of course!" she cried. "Why didn't I think of that before? The robber is about to be unmasked!"

She headed at once for the village.

5

Card Games

Miss Mallard's first stop was at the village drugstore. She showed the receipt to the clerk. He said a code number on the receipt meant that it was for a roll of **gauze**.

"Someone wearing a ski mask

bought that gauze yesterday," said the clerk.

Miss Mallard thanked him and went on to the hardware store. The clerk there said that the other receipt was for a box of plaster.

"See the numbers **'289'** on the receipt?" said the clerk. "That's code for plaster of paris. It was bought yesterday by someone wearing a ski mask."

"Hmmm," said Miss Mallard. She left the hardware store, put on her skis, and was on her way.

Miss Mallard's third stop was at the house where Tilly Pintail was visiting. Tilly's wing was wrapped in gauze. She said that she had burned it while popping popcorn. Miss Mallard told her about the robbery.

"Poor Madam," Tilly said. "She spent all her money to buy that house. The jewels were about all she had left."

Miss Mallard asked Tilly where she had been for the last twelve hours. Tilly claimed she had never left her friend's house.

"Do you play cards?" asked Miss Mallard.

"**Yes!** I love Go Fish and War."

"Hmmm," said Miss Mallard. "Madam Merganser asked me to tell you to return to her house at once."

Miss Mallard left Tilly and went to the house where Chester Gadwall was staying. The first thing she saw there was a box of plaster.

Chester explained that the plaster was being used to mend a

crack in the ceiling. Miss Mallard asked where Chester had been during the last twelve hours. He claimed that he had not gone out of the house. Finally, she asked Chester if he liked to play cards.

"Yes," he answered, "I play Solitaire."

"Hmmm," said Miss Mallard. "Madam Merganser wants you to return to her house at once."

6

Unmasked

With that, she left for the Hotel Edelweiss to see if Philip Merganser was still there.

At the hotel, Miss Mallard learned that Philip Merganser had just gone home by sleigh taxi.

"Poor fellow!" said the hotel's manager. "He checked in yesterday afternoon, just before the storm, with a broken leg. He stayed in his room the whole time with a 'do not disturb' sign on his door."

The manager added, "He left his skis here. I imagine he won't need them for quite a while because of his broken leg."

"I'll take them," said Miss Mallard. "I'm returning now to the Mergansers' house."

Miss Mallard put her skis and Philip Merganser's skis into a sleigh taxi and departed for the Mergansers'. On the way she went through her clipping file.

"Hmmm," said Miss Mallard. "So Philip Merganser also likes to play cards. It says here that he is a **professional** gambler."

When Miss Mallard arrived at the Merganser home, Tilly Pintail opened the door. Tilly took her to the living room.

Inspector Widgeon, Madam

Merganser, and Chester Gadwall were there. So was Philip Merganser, with his leg cast propped up on a footstool.

"Ah, Aunty," said Inspector Widgeon. "I have been waiting for you. What have you found out?"

Miss Mallard looked around the room and said, "I found out that there was no robbery."

"What do you mean?" cried Madam Merganser. "You saw it yourself from the cable car."

"What I saw from the cable

car was a *fake* holdup, Madam," answered Miss Mallard, **"and you know it!** You **plotted** it with someone who is here in this room."

The ducktective continued, "The plan was this: The robber was to make up an **alibi** in the village, ski to your house, and then fake the robbery in front of your window as the cable car went past.

"Then the robber would ski back to the village," Miss Mallard explained, "and hide your jewels. You would wait for the police to come and make out a report so you could collect the **insurance** money on your 'stolen' jewels."

"How dare you!" cried the singer.

"Quiet, Madam," said Inspector Widgeon. "Go on, Aunty."

"The robbery was planned for yesterday," Miss Mallard went on. "The robber came on **schedule**, but then the snowstorm stopped the cable car. Without the cable

car, there would be no **witness** to the crime."

Miss Mallard paused, looked right at Madam Merganser, and added, "So the robber had to wait here overnight until the cable car was running again."

She held up the clues and said, "And these receipts for gauze and plaster and this playing card were all dropped by the robber."

"Not mine," said Tilly Pintail, adjusting her bandage.

"Not mine," said Chester

Gadwall, brushing plaster dust from his sleeve.

"I know," said Miss Mallard. "Only a gambler would need an ace up his sleeve, and you two are *not* gamblers."

She pointed at Philip Merganser and said, "Here is the Ski-Mask Burglar wearing a fake cast made with gauze and plaster of paris."

7

Warm at Last

"Prove it!" Philip Merganser cried.

"All right!" said Miss Mallard. "First, name the doctor who set your leg. Second, explain why your skis were wet when I

brought them from the hotel. And third, why did the hotel manager say that you checked in *before* the storm and not *during* the storm as your wife said?"

All at once, Philip Merganser jumped up and hobbled down the stairs and out the front door, crying, **"You'll never get me!"**

At the same time, his wife let out a scream at the top of her lungs: **AYE-EEEEEEEEEEE!** and there was a roar that sounded like thunder.

Everyone ran outside. A huge clump of snow had fallen off the roof and buried Philip Merganser.

Quickly they pulled him from the snow. As they did, out plopped the jewels from his fake cast.

"Gamblers never win," Miss Mallard said.

"My news clippings mentioned your many gambling **debts**. You and your wife thought you could pay them off with a fake jewel robbery," she told him.

"First, you established an alibi

at the hotel by putting a 'do not disturb' sign on your door. Then you took off your fake cast, slipped out the back door, and came up the mountain. After the fake robbery, you skied back to your room and replaced the cast on your leg," Miss Mallard declared.

"Enough! I give up!" cried Philip Merganser.

"Oh, *why* did it have to be a detective in that cable car!" cried his wife.

"Well done, Aunty, well done,"

said Inspector Widgeon. "But when did you first suspect that the robbery was fake?"

Miss Mallard answered, "Only when I remembered seeing just *one* set of ski tracks in the fresh snow outside the house. That meant the robber had left *after* the storm, because there were no tracks leading *to* the house.

"I deduced—that is, I studied all the clues—that the robber had been here all night and was known to Madam Merganser. But

I had to prove it," she said.

"You're a genius, Aunty," said Inspector Widgeon. "Now let's go inside and warm up before we head back to the village."

"Oh, yes, Willard," said Miss Mallard with a sigh.

Word List

aces (AY·sis): Playing cards that only have one mark that can either be the highest value or lowest

alibi (AL·ih·by): An excuse for not being somewhere

anxiously (ANK·shus·lee): Worried, afraid, or nervous about something

cable car (KAY·bul KAR): A vehicle hanging in the air from a strong cable that is usually pulled up and down a steep slope

catastrophe (kah·TAS·truh·fee): A terrible disaster or event that brings harm

debts (DEHTZ): Something, usually money, owed to a person or bank

gagged (GAGD): Having a piece of cloth put over one's mouth so he or she can't talk

gauze (GAWZ): Thin cotton cloth used to cover a wound

insurance (in·SHUR·entz): Payment paid against accidents

merge (MERJ): Come together to become one thing

plotted (PLAH·ted): Made a secret plan against someone

professional (pro·FESH·uh·nul): Expert at one's job

receipt (ree·SEET): A piece of paper showing the sale of an item

retreat (ree·TREET): A vacation home

schedule (SKEH·jool): A plan of things to be done

witness (WHIT·ness): A person who sees something happen

Questions

1. Which character in this story hates the cold weather?
2. What clues helped Miss Mallard solve the mystery?
3. Who had a skiing accident and broke his or her leg?
4. What card games does Tilly like to play? Which one does Chester like? What card games do you like to play?
5. What was the name of the hotel where Philip Merganser stayed?

Acknowledgments

My thanks and appreciation go
to Jon Anderson, president and
publisher of Simon & Schuster
Children's Books, and his talented
team: Karen Nagel, executive
editor; Karin Paprocki, art director;
Tiara Iandiorio, designer; Elizabeth
Mims, managing editor; Sara Berko,
production manager; Tricia Lin,
assistant editor; and Richard
Ackoon, executive coordinator;
for launching out into the world

again these incredible new editions of my Miss Mallard Mystery books for today's young readers everywhere.